Is a Rotten Apple Still Sweet?

Is a Rotten Apple Still Sweet?

Red Angel

iUniverse, Inc.
Bloomington

IS A ROTTEN APPLE STILL SWEET?

iUniverse books may be ordered through booksellers or by contacting:

iUniverse
1663 Liberty Drive
Bloomington, IN 47403
www.iuniverse.com
1-800-Authors (1-800-288-4677)

ISBN: 978-1-4620-6065-8 (sc)
ISBN: 978-1-4620-6067-2 (hc)
ISBN: 978-1-4620-6066-5 (ebk)

Printed in the United States of America

iUniverse rev. date: 10/26/2011

TABLE OF CONTENTS

Inspirational Passages:
Defining the story, "Is a Rotten Apple Still Sweet?"
Elements of Its creation & In-conclusion

Complementary poems by, author Red Angel;

DEDICATION

I dedicate this book to my two beautiful daughters, "The Angelettes." I want to be an inspiration to them. By setting the example of whatever you want in life, you can accomplish. As long as you believe in yourself and embrace the qualities God designed in you. Power is knowledge, and success is a thought away. Keep the faith serve and glorify our creator. "For we are created by greatness therefore there's nothing less to be expected."

"For I am of the water now I drink of it. For those whom stay in the bottle, will only consume what's in the bottle. I don't know about you but there's enough water on this planet for us all to consume a drink."

A SPECIAL THANK YOU!

~ I most importantly thank God. I thank God for my strength, my courage and my wisdom. I'm grateful for many fruits. I just want God to continue to use me for his glory.

~ I have to thank my Mentor Weusi Olusola. My beloved uncle. Before his transition he requested that I must write my book. He for filled his purpose. He too was a great "Righter", I guess the "Apple didn't fall far from the tree". As he would say, "peace and love."

~ I have to thank my mother Elvira L. Crumpton, and my beloved father Willie F. Clay. I thank them for creating me. And blessing me with their immeasurable love.

~I have to thank my grandmother Estella Clay, for being my blanket. Covering me with protection, wisdom and unconditional love.

~ I must thank my husband for being such a great father. As well as being supportive and patient of me. I appreciate your love, and the knowledge that we share. As for our love, "True love will stand the test of time."

INSPIRATIONAL PASSAGES: DEFINING OF THE STORY CREATION

Going back to the beginning of time. Before we became a part of God's great creations. When the King of the Universe set forth human life and the habitat of its existence. Trees, nature, land and the Lord giveth his right hand to create people. He made us of his likeness. Therefore we are magical, righteous and loving. Love is the key to life treasures. For we all have been designed with many gifts it's up to us key holders to turn the key. Embrace and deceit our light that shines truth and understanding of our true being.

We are all created to glory the light that shines in our essence. It's there for a reason. How you treat yourself and others will determine the manifestation of your season. We are co-creators of the Divine. We are vessels linked into the galaxies. We're of many "Planets." Define PLAN: Definite Purpose. Define NET: To Protect and Shield. With that said we are connected to a "Planet," I suggest we all catch flight fly as high as the sky. Is sky the limit? It's up to you. Explore your galaxy of joy, peace, freedom, truth and most importantly understanding.

Trees are the main ingredient of breathe. Without trees Earth and its entity cannot survive. Trees like us has many purposes. It's oxygen for our sense of smell. It's our fruits for our sense of taste. It's our color for our sense of sight. It's our wind for our sense of touch. It's our ear for the sound that holds nature to hear birds chirping in the air. All things are Divine in the atmosphere. Come close do not fear. Just get to know why you are here.

Apples are like people, they come in many colors. They come from a seed. They come from Earth. They too need trees to exist. They go through stages. Some are sweet, some are sour and some are even Rotten. For we are living in this life of what was created by our ancestors. We have the heart for good that comes natural. And at times the mind of bad that comes from temptations of the flesh. It's all formed into an internal and eternal test.

"Is a Rotten Apple Still Sweet?" This book gives you the opportunity to look in many realities of lives of whom seek pleasure for their unearthly good. Therefore they were handed many challenges of stages like some apples. Some look good on the outside and have a rotten core on the inside. Some look good on the inside and appear rotten on the outside. The seed comes from a good place it's our decisions that flows grace or defoul our face.

This story is written to inspire readers to set high expectations on their lives. Use this story not only as good entertainment. But as an example and to be a life lesson from literature, and not self-experience. Promoting self awareness. We all been through circumstances in our lives that's caused for growth. Let's educate our beings and open up to righteous for our element of intelligence. For power is knowledge and knowledge is power. Allow knowledge to be your protection mechanism.

IN-CONCLUSION

"Is a Rotten Apple Still Sweet?" Is a short story novel, for mature readers. A young lady name Raven is the main character. Her story is inspiring by finding her way out of the bottom of the barrel. She will sprout into the fruits that was always meant for her. This story is relatable to many realities, of women whom experienced tragic domestic abuse. "Everything happens for a reason." Often in life we have to go through the dark to see the light. She was very naïve, also she lacked self confidence and self love. Because of the apples she chose neglected nutrients from the seeds. Her woman hood was challenged of her growing her own seeds. There are elements incorporated of how a young man failed, from the choices and the seeds that he planted. Their harvest lead them to fruits of deception. This story was inspired from the heart and looking into the windows, of many young black men and women lives. The author wants to use her blessings of creativity to enlight ones, mind, decisions and hearts. Her structure of writing reflects her as a "Righter," formality of a writer.

CHAPTER ONE

How Raven Copes From The Loss Of Her Mother.

On July 17, 1979 that was the day I entered this world. My name is Raven Nicole Johnson. I was born at St. Joseph's hospital in Louisiana. I lived with my mother and father in a small shoot gun style house in the city of New Orleans. The exterior of our house was of a faux red brick. We had two bedrooms, my room was pink and white. I had a flock of dolls. My favorite doll of them all was my rag doll. I called her Annie. She reminded me of myself. She had stringy curly hair. Her rosy cheeks featured little splashes of freckles across them. I dragged that doll everywhere I went. My mother had recently bought it for my seventh birthday.

Although our home was small it had a basement that my father used for his band to practice. My father Ervin Johnson Jr, was a talented musician. He played the saxophone for a jazz band, the "Knights of Rhythm," in a small town in Louisiana. I often had trouble sleeping. Because the walls would liberate of vibrations from all the sensation of my father's music. His drum set was midnight blue, with a shiny chrome microphone with the stand to match. Boy, I remember how much I got yelled at for playing with that microphone. I thought I was Mildred Jones. He kept his saxophone put up in a brown case. My father would stay up at all peak hours of the day practicing his music. He had big dreams of making it in the entertainment industry.

My parents relationship was like a rollercoaster. Up and down. I have to admit when it was up, it was great! But when it was down my mother was damaged goods. She didn't handle stress well. My mother Gloria Johnson was my best friend. Her pain frequently affected my feelings. When my mother hurt I hurt. At times I felt myself resenting my father for his unworthy nature. My dad was a womanizer. He was a fairly attractive man, light skin with big light brown eyes. His frame was rather petite. He was slim and short. Back then light skin brothers was in demand. He utilized his looks and his talent to capture erotic women.

My mother had a plaintive sympathetic nature. She wore her heart on her "sleeves." She was not good at camouflaging her dis-ease. She was never close to her family. Because she was a poignant victim of in-sex. She allowed her heart to be heavy. She never forgave her grandfather for fathering her. She was looked upon as a disgrace in the eyes of her family. She was always paranoid that people knew her forbidden secret. My mother was a creole women, that embraced her culture. She was a stellar beauty. She had tan brown skin. Her head flowed of black wavy long locks. Her lips was full and distinctive. Her nose was skinny and narrow. She was classified as a brick house. Everybody said I was her twin.

I found great pleasure in her creole dishes. My favorite dish was her Cajun gumbo. My mother was amazed from my tolerable taste buds for spicy food. She thought I was a bit young to process the spicy flavors. I love spicy food thanks to my mother. Because she made it so altruistically good. Not to mention her key lime pie, was gratifying. She lost touch with her family when she met my father. My parents married after six months of knowing each other. Four months later I was born. My mom was eighteen when she had me. My mother was a run away. She was only seventeen when they got married. My grandmother was surpassingly strict on my mother. She feared her being raped, like her. She tried isolating my mother but it made her escape at her first exit. Meeting my father was my mother's ticket to freedom. My dad was my mom's first companion. His appealing appearance, smooth talk and enchanting charm sold her heart. She instantly fell in love.

My mother was ashamed of her father. I assumed it was her grandfather. I remember my mother being on the phone with her baby sister Ellen. She was the only relative my mother discreetly stayed in contact with. I only met her through phone conversations. I believe My aunt Ellen was also a product of in-sex. I over heard my mother on the phone with my aunt crying and sharing pain. They shared pain of growing up in torture, shame and physical and verbal abuse from their mother. Their mom made then pay the price for her own grandfather's indecency.

My mother was a very sweet lady that loved very hard. Although we didn't have a lot. I never wanted for anything. She was a jack of all trades. A talented beautician and she had a gift for sewing. She made stunning costumes for my father and his band. Their favorite was a silver and gold two piece pants and vest, made of sequin and satin. Holidays I got to wear my gorgeous siphon and lace dresses with beautiful satin bows. All custom made by no one other than my mother. She'll comb my hair with water and grease and tie satin ribbons in my hair to match my dress. My dad and I was all she knew.

My mother was extremely spiritual. She collected angels. Our living room was filled with angelic knick knacks. Pictures of white horses with wings hung upon the walls. The television stand held white candles in a tall clear glass. Every Sunday she'll burn a white candle for a peace offering. She loved reading the bible. She didn't go to church much, she claimed it was full of the beast. Her grandfather was a minister.

My father was arrogant and self centered. He was an aggressive user. He used women for money, even his own family for money. My father's parents lived in Ohio. They came to visit once a year to see me. They really cared a great deal for me. I was their only grandchild. My dad only had one sibling, my aunt Jill. My grandparents was eagerly annoyed with my dad. He took advantage of their fortunate life style that they earned together. He also was an impulsive liar. He'd even use me to swindle money from his parents. He'll lie and say I need money for school, clothes and etc. Whatever it took for him to get his desires. He desired women, drugs, money and music.

My mother was his personal puppet. She gave him whatever his heart yearned for. She cooked and cleaned the house daily. She constantly made a variety of clothes for him. She made him tailored suits, dress shirts and costumes for him and his band mates. Also back then guys was rocking the perm with pumped waves. Of course my father had her do not only his hair, but also his other four band mates hair every week. My mom traveled with my dad and his band. They'll sometimes book three gigs a night. They even hit up after hour clubs to promote their music.

That's when crack cocaine came into her life. My dad introduced it to her. Because it was his drug of choice to be more proactive, alert and awake for long nights of entertainment. He constantly got into fights with my mother about his music. She often accused him of being with other woman. I'll hear her yell at my father saying," you slut of a man." "You've better not bring nothing home you can't get rid of." My dad always was disrespecting her. His common saying to her was, "woman you better be glad you still get it." He was beyond arrogant.

He spent many nights away from home using his music as an excuse. But when he came home moneyless, my mom would become livid. She looked through his clothes pockets and found crack pipes and dust of cocaine. She knew he was sleeping with other woman and getting high off that "shit," she'll call it. I adored my mother. She read me a bed time story every night. My favorite was five little monkeys jumping on the bed. Everyday I would restyle all five of my baby dolls hair imitating my mother. She'll fuss at me for, wasting hair grease in baby dolls hair. My mother always envisioned me and her owning our own hair salon.

My dad worked for a company driving a truck delivering bread during the day. He hated working for the "Man." He pursued his entertaining career with everything he had inside of him. My mom and I was inseparable. I could talk to her about anything.

I asked her what made her name me Raven. She replied, "you're like an intelligent, beautiful black bird." "One day I will get the opportunity to watch your wings grow, and you will fly."

Growing up in my early child hood was very lonely. I remained the only child. My mom said she don't think she could have any more children. My father was satisfied with just me. He didn't care for children that much. In fact I was amongst adults primarily throughout my early child hood. People told me I had an old soul. My vocabulary was acute and spoke of wisdom. Things I would say would spark your internal flame. My internal was glorious. I had my mother genes to thank for that.

My mother always had high expectations for me. She always said, "someday Raven you are going to leave your footprints on the earth's surface." "You will change lives!" My parents friends who did have children never brought them around. They just came to our house to, hang out get high and talk grown people talk. I had a thing for dancing. My nickname was "boogie bones." There wasn't a bone in my body that couldn't boogie. I'd collected many dollars entertaining my parents company.

When my mom and dad both hung out doing music, I had to go to old lady Walker house. She lived just two houses down from me. Ms. Walker was a bundle of joy. She loved to pick apples from the tree and make fresh apple cider. Yummy! I enjoyed swinging from the tire that was roped onto the tree in her backyard. It was near her vegetable garden.

I befriended nature because my street was filled with elderly residents. I played with kids only when I went to school. School was cool. I got to show off my fancy wardrobe in delighted effort of my mother. My fondest memory of school, was riding the yellow school bus. I found it exciting and amusing. Kids loud laughing and playing. Hearing the bus door open, bus stop after bus stop. When it came to my stop my mother was patiently awaiting my arrival. Nature called for my aspiration. What a joy I found in chasing butterflies. Feeding squirrels, watching birds bathe. Listening to the birds chirp. My favorite insect was lady bugs and caterpillars, they were usually found near Ms. Walker's garden. Although I never had anyone to play with at home, nature kept me occupied.

Ms. Walker was like the grandmother I never knew. She was a short fair skin lady, with flowing long grey straight hair. Although her nationality was white, her voice and soul came off as if she was of colour. She had a heavy raspy voice that carried. She wore long short sleeve dresses, with black ankle boots. Everybody respected Ms. Walker. She was a loner all she had was three cats. One cat was black with white spots his name was Cow. Because he ate like one. The other cat was grey, his name was Shadow because he followed her everywhere she went. The last cat was black and his name was Sable. Because he was a black beauty. He was my favorite of them all. Whenever I was sad Sable seemed to sense my distress.

Unfortunately my mom and dad stayed into it. Their fights went from verbal to physical. I noticed bruises on my mother's body. She always took offense for my father's abuse. She would always blame the alcohol or stress to reverence my father's irrational behavior. She prayed so hard for God to make things better. She was in love, blind and didn't want to see. She later became a dead man walking.

I spent many nights with Ms. Walker she enjoyed my company. She felt sorry for me. My mother and I was growing further away. Now that my dad is gone. He left my mother for an older white woman with money. He came around just to check in every once in a while. My mom pain was corrupting her being. She transitioned into a deep depression and spent many nights drinking, smoking and shooting her arms with that poison. She was heartbroken. She literally gave up on life. I told myself, "when I grow up and get a man, I vow to never let a man bring me down!"

Later that fall my mother felled into an even deeper depression. I noticed her complexion was becoming more pale. Her brick house frame, began to mold into a stick house. She was withering away. My father check in's came to an end. Once he signed onto permanent gigs for his music tour, and made a name for his self. I didn't miss him much we rarely communicated. On a fall Saturday afternoon my mother asked Ms. Walker to watch after me. She claimed she had some important errands to make. She said she's not sure when she'll be back. She gave Ms. Walker my grandparents contact information in Ohio.

My mother graciously thanked Ms. Walker for being such a great help and care taker for me. My mother then turned and looked at me with a shake to her spirit from nerves and said, "always know I love you." "And no matter how far we are, we'll always be close in heart." She then gave me an explosive hug and kiss. She began to cry and I heard her whisper, "I'm tired baby, I'm ready to go." "You be a good girl for me." "I love you." My mom felt she wasn't giving me what I needed. All her energy was exalted. Therefore she felt I would be better off without her. I never seen my mother so deathly depressed. I was only seven years old I didn't comprehend what my mother was truly expressing. She was voicing me her last words. That Saturday night my mother never showed up.

Sunday afternoon I was just awaking from a nap. I grabbed my doll Annie. Then me and Ms. Walker proceeded to look for my mom. We walked down to my house. When we looked in the house my mom had her white candles burning. Music was playing the record was "Long Time Coming." We looked in her room. All we saw was her window opened with the fall breeze moving her bedroom white lining curtains back and forth. I then shut the window.

While walking through the living room, I glanced at the bathroom. There she was lying on the bathroom wooden floor covered with blood. She was lifeless. Her eyes was crocked back into her head, and blood gushing from her arms pierced with needles. She had O.D, her head was near the end of the tub. She was only twenty five years old. I cried and screamed while Ms. Walker held me in her submission.

She then called the ambulance and took me in. She called around to people that knew my father. Finally my father's parents was contacted and sent for me. My mother was cremated and her ashes was spread into the waters of a small lake near a creek, Ms. Walker took me to. I was numb for a while.

CHAPTER TWO

Raven Grandparents Gains Guardianship.

My grandparents open their lives up to me. Their hearts was made of gold. They planted love seeds on me like never before. They was so happy to have me. I was like their little girl. They said I will keep them young. My grandparents names was Ervin and Nancy Johnson. They both were in their late fifties at that time. They work as Forman's at a commercial industrial plant. People often referred to them as brother and sister. Because they both awfully favored one another. They were a cute couple. Both had light yellowish toned skin. Nice grades of hair. My grandfather had silver hair with a high top fade. He had small eyes with a round big nose. His lips was extremely thin. He was very laid back. He enjoyed the finer things in life. He wore all kinds of high end designer clothes, watches and colognes. He was a snappy sharp dresser.

My grandmother was light as well with big almond shape eyes, with a pointed nose and thick lips. She part took of the glitz and glamour lifestyle as well. She had diamond incrusted rings, tennis bracelets. She wore at least five different necklaces at one time. She looked like "Mr. T." She was allured by my talent of hair styling. She loved rocking french rolls. I faithfully did her hair every other week. They both had youthful personalities. They both drove fancy cars. My poppy had a black 500 class Mercedes Benz. My grandmother drove a white Jaquar. They complemented each other quite well. The way they treated one another was like the blueprint of happiness, family and marriage. Their house was a two story brick colonial. They lived in a suburban subdivision in Toledo Ohio.

Our block was filled with kids. That's how I met my best friend Alyssa Wilson. She looked black and Chinese. She was darker brown skinned. With smaller features she had a little button nose. She had small bubble lips with little beattie eyes. She lived next door to me. Her grandmother was raising her. We had a lot in common. Her mom was alive but she rarely seen her. Because she was a drug abuser. Her dad, she never met. She had an older sister name Debbie that was five years older than us.

We grew extremely close, we were like sisters. She was always over my house, and I was always over her house. We shared clothes and we loved to dress alike. She was the sheer queen. She'll cut up jeans into multiple designs and shirts. I on the other hand was the hair stylist. I did our hair in the same styles. We both had shoulder length hair hers was just black and mine was medium brown. People thought we really were sisters. We always had each other back.

I remember on a hot August summer day we both had just recently turned twelve years old. Her birthday was in June and mine was in July. We had on black biker shorts with a neon pink stripe going down the side on the shorts. We wore long neon pink t shirts with a knot tied on the side of our hips. Our shoes were some fresh crisp white pumpkin seeds. We both had on pink and black slouch socks to match. Our hair was up in a fan pony tail on top of our heads, surrounding pink and black thick pony tail holders. Our bangs was curled upwards and flipped to one side of our face.

We both were riding our bikes in the neighborhood. We discovered a festival going on down at one of the churches. They we're having a youth day celebration for all the local kids and were giving away school supplies. We decided to go. We got to play different games. We even won some prizes. The festival also was running a marathon, that a lot of twelfth graders were participating in. One of the seniors was a guy name Calvin. I had a major crush on him before I ever met him. How could I forget that face. I noticed it in Alyssa's sister Debbie's year book. I find myself drooling over his captivating fine appearance.

The next day me and my best buddy went for a walk. We walked around the corner talking boy talk. As I was talking about my crush why was he sitting in his sky blue 1979 Monte Carlo supreme, tented windows with custom rimes. His music was punching through the speakers. He stop me and Alyssa as we walked. He tried to holler at me, until he found out I was only twelve years old. Alyssa big mouth of course, she yelled out, "jail bate." He thought I was at least fifthteen years old. He then told me that I was a little cutie. Then stated, "In five years you'll be ready!" I got to really get a good look at him this time it was the real deal.

He was picture perfect. His skin was carmel, his hair was black with thick waves covering his crown. His lips were medium thick. He had dreamy eyes. His mustache was thin and fine. I truly was in love with him. He smelled so good. It was getting towards the end of the summer. My love was getting ready to go to college. I made Alyssa help me come up with a way to see him, just once more.

We were outside sitting on her porch, and the paper boy was out delivering paper. Alyssa opened the paper, what do you know. Right on the front page there was an article about "Calvin Cook." He was slam dunking on the basketball court. He attended Carter High school he had a promising college basketball career ahead of him. When Alyssa told me he was in the paper, I thought she was pulling my leg. Alyssa said, "that's it!" I replied. "what?" She said, "well we can walk around the corner and see if he's home, and have him sign his autograph." I felt happy and shy. I pulled myself together and Alyssa and I went on our little walk.

There he was just pulling into his drive way. He got out the car wearing an all white Nike track suit. With some all white crispy air force ones. Wearing his gold two inch hearing bone chain, with a scorpio charm on it. His wrist was incrusted with a gold diamond Rolex. He was spoiled rotten rumor has it. His dad was a dope dealer. He saw us walking pass his house. He said, "what's up little wifey." I replied, "you!" "Mr. Basketball Star." I then showed him the paper. He didn't even know he made headlines. He was impressed. I then asked him to sign his name, as I was a fan. He went to his car and got a blue ink pen. He signed my paper reading, "stay sweet and pretty, your boy Calvin "Cook", cause you know I be smoking on the courts!".

That night before I went to bed I sniffed that paper a hundred times it smelled good like him. I placed the paper under my pillow before I went to sleep. Sweet dreams. I needed it. I every once in a blue moon would have vicious nightmares of the vision of my mother's death. I use to cry and run into bed with my granny and poppy. They even took me to counseling. But somehow I never could escape from the triumph that was caused, from experiencing my mother's death hands on.

I'm now a seventeen year old senior at Carter High school. Growing up without my parents hasn't been easy. I must say I'm pretty grateful to have such caring, loving and supportive grandparents. I pretty much get whatever I want, and can do almost anything I want. I was a fortunate young lady. My granny and poppy both is now retired from one of the industry's largest automotive companies. They also own various rental properties, and is financially well off.

High school has been quite an adventure and growing experience. I must admit, I've became more popular in the eyes of the guys. I always knew I was fairly attractive. But I was very modest, naïve, and somewhat insecure of my luscious lips. I would constantly lick my lips and hold them tight to portray a smaller appearance, of my fuller lips. All of my self-conscious parts of my outer appearance were finally coming together for me to appreciate them.

Even with that said I still feel somewhat vulnerable and incomplete. I never could seem to get over the death of my mother. I felt so empty and a huge void of love. I've always thought my mother never really loved me. Because she wouldn't of killed herself. I don't go a day without having mind trickling nightmares of the image of my mother. Lying dead eyes rolled back. Blood gushing from her head, and her arms were pieced with needles. I still to this day hold a grudge against my father. He basically killed my mother and her dreams. Because of him she will never get to share my life with me. He has stolen all my dreams of having a mother. My father always told me how I look just like my mother, and how I'm so much like her.

Although I was only seven years old when she died. For some reason I still feel her presence. I just don't know how, but somehow I do know she watches over me. My father never was the standup type he relied on his parents to raise me. Yeah he sent birthday cards every so often and a call here and there. But eventually it stopped once his head lied on the promiscuous soles of loose women.

My aunt Jill was my dad's one and only sibling. She lived in Manhattan, New York. She visited every so often. She was a very talented Lawyer that was always on the move. She was single and enjoyed her lifestyle of high prestige and privileges. She didn't have any children. I admired her she was a very beautiful, independent, and intelligent black woman. Her lips were big and beautiful like mine. Her hair was mid back length and cold black. Her complexion was of fair skin. It was a light that shined through her, as bright as the sunshine. Her eyes could spark up a star in the sky. She always looked fly, with her head held high.

Every time she came to visit, she always took me shopping and out to eat where they served lavish cuisines. She wanted to set my life expectations high. She noticed I was a bit insecure and lacked self-confidence. She wanted me to feel beautiful, and know I was beautiful. My aunt Jill was impressed with my talent of practicing, "Hair Styling." She stated it was a good hustle. She said, "make sure whatever you do, rather It's a Doctor, Lawyer or a Hair Stylist." "If a Hair Stylist you be the best Hair Stylist and make history."

My aunt was always happy, confident and secure I wished she lived here. Although she lived far away she always kept me close to heart. Every birthday and holiday she remembered me. I guess she made up for all the birthdays and holidays my dad missed. My fondest memory of my mother was she was a talented beautician. She was the, "Hair Stylist of the town." I loved watching her do her. I always wanted to be just like her. I guess I should be careful what I say because, I don't know if that will be a "gift" or a "curse."

CHAPTER THREE

Raven Finds Love.

While attending Carter High school I gravitated on maturity quickly. I was inflicted by peer pressure. I then became closer to a young lady name Michelle. She was fast as lightening. She smoked weed, cigarettes and drank. I met her in the girls bathroom in tenth grade. She was smoking a cigarette, just coming from the boys bathroom.

She was letting a boy name Trey, "feel her up." She was a lot thicker than average. But she had a really pretty face. She wore her hair in a bob dyed red with black streaks. At the time I had my hair in a shoulder length wrap with blonde and brown streaks. She wanted to know who did my hair, She was appalled that I did my very own hair. My hair witnessed of a professional appearance. It had grace of body, neatness and texture.

Michelle wasn't Alyssa's cup of tea. She wasn't into rebel type of individuals. I found Michelle's personality vibrant and never boring. We started to hang out a little more than Alyssa and I.

Alyssa was very book smart and was always concentrating on her studies. She was getting closer to her boyfriend, Darwin. They did complement each other well. Darwin was cute. He was not that tall. But he looked half Asian and black. His eyes were small every time he smile his eyes would disappear. He had black shiny hair with thick natural waves. The school voted them the couple of the year. They then were going into their second year of going steady. They acted old and married. She was becoming vague.

Although her and Darwin was closer than a twin pop. She still found time to squeeze in a hair appointment. She was still my best friend we just was growing into our own personalities. She was one of my freebies. She never had to pay to get her hair done. We still kicked it every once in a while. But I found Michelle being fun to be around and funny. She cursed like a sailor. And told jokes from the top of her head, that set well with every conversation.

She was in a state of shock when she found out, I was still a virgin. Everyday she'll jokenly ask me, "girl did you get you some yet?" We would just fall out laughing. She always told me, "girl you keep hanging around me I'm gone find yo ass some." Mind you we were only fifteen at the time. She already had not one but two abortions. She told me her older sister from her dad's side, vulcher as her guardian. To hide the pregnancies from her mother. She was always skipping school. She dated a lot of older guys some even late twenties. I asked her did they know how old she was. She'll reply, "most know and don't care!" She then said that guys got off on the fact of her age. I'm starting to realize in many people hearts that bad was good.

One morning before they opened the doors to our school. Michelle was at the corner talking to a guy in an older Chevy truck. It was brown with dub rimes shining on the wheels. She waved for my attention and called me over. That's how she met quite of few of her flings, was from right outside of the school. I proceeded to walk over and the passenger was a very dark guy with corn rolls. He had a blunt tucked behind his ear. He looked like he was at least twenty years old. Michelle was talking to the driver. She was trying to get me to skip school with her I was objective. Only because Alyssa was watching my every move. I didn't want Alyssa seeing me leave with her. She already thought Michelle was a bad influence. That situation would of been her validation.

The next day at school Michelle bragged about how good the weed was and how high she got. She wanted me to go with her the following day to hang out with the same guys. She implied on how the guy that was trying to pursue me was paid. We planned to skip school the following day. We indeed met at the gas station across the street from school. Before we walked in the gas station to buy some gum. I was looking down in my purse. Michelle uttered, "all shit!" I replied, "What?" The police rode right up on the both of us. At that time the law was school hours all students are to be in the school facility. Those whom was skipping didn't have a chance. The police was adamant on their mission of, picking up skipping students. They weren't buying Michelle's excuse of her having a headache and was buying aspirins. We both were on our way to jail. We had to wait hours before we could call our guardians.

We grew extremely hungry. Michelle big Ms. Hard Ass, started crying like a baby. She had enough meat on her you'll think could preserve her for a while. I on the other hand was thinking about how my grandparents was going to react. I said to myself I should of listened to Alyssa. This girl was a ball of fire. She wasn't worried about getting into trouble. She had a gang of family members that pledged her wrong doings. Her people showed her love in an immoral way. I was brought up differently. I was raised to have morals. I think that's why she did the things she did. Because you only know what you're taught. She lacked real love, and didn't know any better. If she did she just didn't care. Her mind was fried.

In the jail cell she expressed to me, how her mother always had different men. How the men was running in and out of her home. Michelle expressed how she was an early developer. Men always took her for being a grown woman. She revealed how her mother's boyfriend's friend was cute. She allowed him to take her virginity when she was thirteen. Her mother found out and beat her like she was a woman off the street. Michelle then said, "It was her fault in the first place." She went on and said how she was allowed to smoke weed with her mother. I was outrageously shocked! She said, "my mother would rather me smoke with her." "Then to smoke with strangers, with the risk of getting my weed laced." She said now, "I'm addicted to weed and sex." Every since then she looked for men to be her outlet, to express temporary affection.

My grandmother always told me not to grow up too fast. She often said, "once your grown you'll always be grown." "You're only a child for a little while." Finally it's now 4 pm in the afternoon. My grandparents came and picked me up. That's when they got to meet Michelle. My grandparents both can look at Michelle and tell she is trouble. By the way she carried herself they instantly could tell she was loose. Michelle was a full size girl and was top heavy and always managed to wear shirts that exposed her cleavage. I was forbidden to talk to Michelle. She use to call my house using another name, "Lisa."

One day she begged for me to do her hair. She had a "hot date, can't be late!" I asked my granny if I could do her hair. She finally gave in. I charged $15—$25 per style. Depending on the detail and the time put into the hair style determined the price. While I was doing her hair my grandmother offered her some apple cobbler. It was infectiously delicious.

My grandmother had a little salon area, set up for me in our basement. It was a little room painted purple and white. I had a black salon chair, with a mirror station with bright light bulbs shining down on a ton of hair sheens, shampoos, conditioners, combs, brushes and etc. I also had little capes for my clients. I even had a hair dryer chair. My granny hooked me up with my very own private salon.

During my high school years, I incorporate my passion for hair. I no longer could think about skipping. Let alone a boyfriend. Being a virgin is not so bad after all. After talking to Michelle last night. I discovered sex can definitely wait! Michelle revealed to me a concern. She was frightened, she caught a STD! Yikes! I was scared for her. She wasn't in school the next day. When school was over I went home right away to call her. She told me she went to the free clinic. She had to get a shot. She was given a prescription of antibiotic to treat chlamydia. With school and doing hair I was pretty occupied.

I never judged people. I befriend Michelle because, of her outgoing personality. I always felt like people are the way they are because of what they been through. Most experiences are made for growth. Our friendship balanced one another. She made me smile. I made her think. I guess it's true the opposite does attract. I made a boat load of money towards my last year of high school. Like my mother I became the, "Hair Stylist of my school district."

Word passed fast, in reference to my hair styling abilities. I was getting more business, then I could handle. But the money was grand. I embraced the expensive taste that I was subjected to. I would clean up off of money made from homecomings, proms, and dances. I'm now a senior on wheels. I actually saved up for my very first car. Of course my grandparents matched my savings. I bought a pre-owned 2door sports addition Ford Probe it was candy apple red.

I enjoyed picking up my friends from school. Going to the mall and just hanging out. I've always been picky when it came to the fella's. I only had a couple of boyfriends once in the 8th grade, and once in the 10th grade a guy name Hakeem we dated a while nothing super special. I liked extremely attractive guys with soft hair, smaller lips and a muscular physique.

On a spring Saturday afternoon my friend Tasha and I decided to go to a Youth Center to swim. And that's when I met a guy by the name of Calvin. Calvin was in the basketball auditorium. When Michelle and I walked passed getting ready to go to the pool. Calvin and I locked eyes. He was a tall glass of water standing 6 feet even, and 185 pounds all muscle. Chestnut brown skin, with natural curly locks on the top of his head. He was wearing a red t-shirt, black gym shorts with red and black Jordan's on his feet. He even had the nerve to have some bling too. He had a nice 2 carat earrings in both ears. A turkish linked necklace with an iced out cross around his neck. Calvin had the most sexiest thin mustache, goatee and side burns to die for. He was the epiphany of my, "dream man."

Calvin yelled out "light skin!" My friend Tasha is medium brown, short petite with oval shaped eyes, short Toni Braxton styled hair with a dark side to her. That day Michelle didn't want to hang out with us. She felt Tasha was competition. They both shared the same demoralized behaviors. When Calvin yelled out, "light skin" loudly again. Tasha replied, "girl you better push up on that!" So I told him to come to me and we exchanged names and numbers. I looked at the paper he wrote his name and telephone number on. His name read Calvin. I did a double take look at him. I couldn't believe my eyes. It was my crush!

After all the reminiscing, day dreaming, wishing and fantasizing of him. The manifestation had reach its cycle, In the universe. My grandmother most favorable saying was, "be careful what you ask for." "Make sure it's what you want." "You may get what you may not want !" Calvin was tripping he exclaimed, "you the little momma that lived next door to Debbie?" I replied, "yep!" He said, "you all grown up now." "You filled out wonderfully."

I was ready for him on site. My modest ass even had the nerve to do a full turn around for him. While my body infectious hair was swinging in the air. I was wearing tight blue jeans with a baby t. My boobs got firm and rigid from the excitement of seeing him.

Calvin's friend Russ short for Russell came up to Tasha and they started talking. Russ was a lot shorter than Calvin. His skin was light brown with flaws of acne. He had rough hair he kept in a bold fade. His facial hair was of a compact textured. He had big droopy eyes. His lips was small and a bit ashy. His teeth had a noticeable over bit. He looked as if he sucked his thumb a lot when he was younger. He still pulled girls because he had money.

Both Calvin and Russ asked if they could join us in the pool. I was indeed gamed. We all swamped and flirted for a while. I was feeling this brother, we felt mad chemistry from the beginning. When Tasha and I was wrapping up and our way. Calvin and Russ insisted on inviting us to Calvin's apartment. I quickly responded to accept his invitation. By my grandparents being elder, I can come and go as I please. As long as checked in every once in a while to inform them of my doings and where about. Now that I've proved myself to them and earned back trust. In my grandparents eyes I was an "Angel." Tasha on the other hand had a curfew of 10:30 pm.

Once we all got back to Calvin's place he played some Hip Hop music and rolled up some joints, and had a fifth of Hennessy already set up for females to indulge. Tasha fast ass knew all about that stuff for she had some experience if you know what I mean. She was quite the, "in girl." The fella's was use to "getting in", sort of speak with her. I knew what the guys was up to, "Booty Call!" I just took it in as a self freedom and growing up pilot. I knew what I was getting myself into. I just let moments take its place. I was drawn to "bad girls." Their ways was finally rubbing off on me.

My first mind was very apprehensive and timid about the whole drinking and smoking situation. But the attraction I had for Calvin was so physically strong I played along with his game. Therefore we all began laughing and dancing. All while consuming drinking and smoking. As the evening evolved Calvin kept kissing me on my neck. He was telling me how beautiful I was. His lips felt so internally good, along with his touch as he caress my breast and butt. I keep playing it off as if I didn't want him to be so affectionate, but my body wanted more. My mind at this point didn't exist. I just wanted Calvin to take me however he wished.

Tasha and Russ was already in Calvin's guest room, doing god knows what. Calvin looked me straight in my eyes, and asked me "what was up?' I knew in my mind that meant panties staying up or down. I was feeling pretty buzzed after getting contact from the weed smoke. I never cared for smoking I made it up on my share of glasses of Hennessy.

We entered his room, it was dark and it smelled like fresh cool water cologne. My heart was racing. I thought it was going to pop out of my chest. I was pleased to see he practiced safe sex. He placed the condom on his rather crass male utensil of pleasure. I was in heaven, it was my first time getting my fancy tickled if you know what I mean.

I felt myself having an outer body experience. I had waterfalls draining from my vagina on to my inner thighs. He slowly penetrated me, for he could tell it was my first time. He gently broke into my flesh. It was what I always imagined and then some. That was the best sex that I ever had literally. I was whipped, at least I could admit it. He instructed me how to do him. He taught me many sexual pleasures. Boy was he a great instructor. At this time I didn't care that I just met him. Because our attraction was so strong we didn't try to fight the feeling we embraced it. I felt we were going to create a long lasting relationship. I truly knew, "I found the one."

After a session of passion and pleasure came to its peak, Tasha knocked on the door. She replied that Russ was getting ready to drop her off at home. It was passed her curfew. Calvin pleaded for me to stay. I must confess I dam sure wasn't ready to leave him. I called home and talked to my granny and told her I was staying the night at a girlfriend's house.

CHAPTER FOUR

The Morning After.

The next morning, when I woke up in my "new mans bed." I thought to myself, I sure do feel like a woman. I felt irresistible, sexy and addicted to Calvin. My thoughts were, I wanted Calvin more then I needed him. Before I could exercise my thoughts of him. Calvin came out of the bathroom fully dressed, and replied he'll be back. He gave me an intimate kiss and made me chew his gum. He then asked for it back. He then replied, "now you know I love yo little ass, you haven't even brushed your teeth." We both burst out laughing. He then looked at me before he walked out of the room and said, "sweet taste." "Just like you."

He was quite a smack talker. He called me his young tender. He was funny, loving, sexy and mine all mines. I dreamt of this moment. So good to be Raven Nicole Johnson. He was worth the wait. He had two cell phones, and he left one for me at that time I only had a pager. I then noticed pictures of him playing basketball for a team in Germany. I also noticed tons of championship awards from Carter high school and San Diego University. His bedroom set was black and gold. He had a king size bed with red satin sheets. His chest dresser, was full of all his trophies, metals, and championship rings. His dresser with the mirror was full of every designer cologne you can think of. I also seen pictures of him holding two little girls and one little boy that resembled him immensely. The pictures was tucked in the frame of his dresser mirror.

After nosing around I decided to shower. Once I showered I went into his closet and put on a white t-shirt. That boy gym shoe game was over the top. I thought I was in Footlocker. I looked in some of his boxes that was on his top shelve. He had pictures of different women. He was a freak. But he's my freak now. After looking at the pictures. I can contest that some of the women on those pictures was not "pretty." They was average. They had nothing on me. I peeked into another box on the top shelf and notice a black nine mill-meter glock. Scary!

Finally it was time to stop playing peek a boo. Therefore I put on some of his deodorant and powder. That I got off of his dresser. I pulled out the very first drawer towards my right looking for socks. What do you know I found another "box." Shall I look? You bet I did. I found some weed in a sandwich size bag. I also found a distributor bag size of little white rocks. I assumed the rocks were for his distributing purposes. "Any who," too bad my panties was hand washed and hanging up on the bathroom shower rod drying. I may have been panty less, but I was floating on cloud nine.

To help the time pass I watched T.V. And before I was getting ready to put on a video. Calvin called me and asked me what I wanted to eat. He picked up burgers and fries. Before I knew it we both were eating and talked for hours. He told me he was my man officially. He knew I attended the same high school as him. He emphasized, that he still knew some people that attended my high school.

Calvin asked if I knew a guy name Cliff, Stan, and Rocky. I told him, I didn't really kick it with that many people. I keep to myself for the most part. Guys tried to holla but my taste is very limited. I told him I did know of "Rocky." Rocky played football, that's how I knew him. Calvin got on the phone and called a few of the guys, and asked about me. They all said I was fine as hell. They called me a stuck up pretty girl. He announced to them, that I was his woman. He gave them the permission to put the smash down on anyone that tried to mess with me in any kind of way.

Calvin kept saying, you're going to make me lose out on some money today." Because he wanted to spend the rest of his day with me. Therefore I knew in the back of my mind he was a street hustler. Plus because of my earlier detective actions. I just wanted to hear it from him. I wanted him to tell me his story. I knew he was older and mature. I found his mystery magical. So far I know he's five years older than me. He played basketball overseas. He makes me feel out of sight. He got some money and he's digging me. At this time what more can a girl ask for. Oh, plus he's fine.

The following weekend I spent with Calvin getting to know one another. He told me playing basketball overseas, didn't work out. Because he caught a case, in which he didn't levirate on. He also told me, he has twin daughters Kelly and Kate Lynn 2 years old. The girls live with their mother Sharon back in Detroit Michigan. Sharon is 3 three years older than Calvin. He claims she has a man. He also claimed to be an active dad.

This was a Thursday therefore I missed school for that day. I played it off to my granny that I was doing a school science presentation. I needed to stay the night with my lab partner. My lie was not holding up so well after waiting, for Russ. Russ took my car last night when he dropped off Tasha. I haven't seen or heard from him until late that evening. When he walked in Calvin's apartment. Calvin went postal on him. Finally I made it home. My granny wasn't mad. She took my word. I was shocked that I wasn't in trouble. Things was looking and feeling tremendously good for me.

I immediately rushed to the phone and contacted Michelle. When she answered the phone she said, "hello." I answered back and said, "what up though?!" She knew something was up because of my intro. We laughed until our stomach hurt. She exclaimed, "bitch you got you some!" She then replied, "who is he, was it good and when do I get to meet him?" The following day was a Friday. I managed to get to stay the weekend with my "lab partner." Finals was coming up, therefore my granny allowed me to stay over for the weekend.

That weekend Calvin and I became better acquainted. I was thrown for a loop. Calvin was a popular guy. He had girls calling him left and right. As well as his guy friends trying to see if he was coming out to the "bar." Calvin was intrigued by strip clubs.

31

He was something else. I figure by the way I put it down on him. He'll eventually change his ways. But as the weekend progressed. I noticed his phone was blowing up none stop. He'll answer and hang up. I was getting irritated.

Calvin then told me he wanted to introduce me to some of his boys. Shortly before he could finish asking me to meet his boys. A big banging fist emerged onto his front door. After all the calls I felt extremely uncomfortable. I didn't know what to expect. It was his boys, Russ and Shamrock. Shamrock was big black and ugly. He stood at least 6 feet 3 inches. Weighing a good three hundred pounds plus. He had a big bald head. He was very intimidating.

The first thing Shamrock said was, "who is this pretty little thick red bone?" Calvin replied, "that's me!" Shamrock replied how much you had to spend to get that one. Calvin quickly corrected Shamrock's gestures. He indicated that I wasn't like "the others." And that I was a good girl. I got the que on how Calvin is. He was hood and hood rich. Russ greeted me in a nice and suddle way. He greeted me with a hug and asked about Tasha. Shamrock immediately followed the response of, "where your girls at that look like you?"

I then called Tasha, Michelle and Alyssa. Tasha couldn't come out she was already on punishment, from the night she was last at Calvin's. Alyssa and Michelle came through. I was so impressed that Alyssa came out. Michelle of course was no surprise. We all agreed on renting movies, getting pizza and making daiquiri's. Michelle and I went to the store to get the mix to make the drinks. Calvin took Alyssa to the video store because she had a membership card. Russ stayed with Shamrock to break down some weed for Calvin. Michelle and I made it back, we began to make drinks.

Calvin and Alyssa still haven't made it back. Michelle starting replying, "they better have some good ass movies." "And that pizza better be the bomb." I wasn't concerned, until they came back and Alyssa had a mortified look on her face. I took her into the bathroom and asked her if she was alright. She just starting crying saying how she missed Darwin. Darwin had left for the weekend to visit colleges down in Tennessee. They never been apart for the last four years now that they've been together. I laughed and said, "oh that's why your butt came out tonight huh!"

She laughed we both expressed how much we missed each other. We all had a goodnight after all. We played domino's, cards, watched movies and ate. It was a blast! Michelle got with Shamrock. They actually hit it off pretty good. She told me she love her some big black brothers with long money. I drove Alyssa back home she gave me a hug and told me to be careful. She then looked at me and said, "I love you, and I'll always be here for you." She told me to take it easy. Have fun and be good.

When I returned back to Calvin's, the pizza was obsolete. Michelle and Shamrock put the mash down on that pizza. The only thing left was the antipasto salad. That night was crazy. Michelle and Shamrock, rocked the house! They both were big, loud, hungry and horny creators. The next morning I heard

Shamrock and Calvin talking about how freaked out Michelle was. I know she was gone from how they were talking about her. I also over hear Shamrock talking about me. He peeked in on me and Calvin while we were sleeping. He saw me in my underwear. He yelled out, "little momma body is banging!" I was so pissed. Fat nasty pervert. I wish he would try something with me. I'll make him choke off of his neck fat.

Back to school, Michelle and I met in the bathroom. She was complimenting me and Calvin. She said, "yall make a cute ass couple." I thanked her and responded, "you and big boy isn't so bad either." She was exclaiming over and over again, "we hit the jackpot!" She then told me that Shamrock gave her $50 and a bag of weed. She asked what has Calvin gotten me. I took his chain from underneath my shirt. She replied, "you his girl!" Because the chain was heavy and expensive. I then told her I'm independent. I don't need a man to pay for me I'm not a prostitute. Michelle relied, "It's not tricking if you got it." That girl was from another world. She was down for whatever.

A lot for a 17 year old to swallow. I began to focused on my schooling and participated in senior extra curriculum activities. I was a part of the debate team because I had thoughts of being a lawyer like my aunt. I started to do some of my grandmother's friends from church hair. My grandmother was so proud to show me off. Granny always told me, "I may not be the prettiest girl in the world but I was one of them."

She thought I was super talented and smart. I did make the honor roll every report card except once in tenth grade. My grandfather paid me graciously whenever I made the honor roll. I was money motivated. My granny was so pleased with my hair talent. Her friends that were my clients was very generous, especially their tips. I thought if I would study more and stay busy I would eventually forget about Calvin. The more I did the more I thought of him. Alyssa and I starting contemplating on what colleges we were going to attend. Alyssa and I got into Tennessee state. She was ecstatic because her twin pop was going there. She tried so hard convincing me to attend college there. She was interested in criminal justice and nursing. I wasn't sure of what school I was attending, nore what career path I was taking.

My senior year came up on me so fast. All I use to do was concentrate on my studies and doing hair. Now I have a boyfriend. I do what grown people do. I was going up faster than I anticipated at the time. I started to fear my future of uncertainty. My boo now gives me air room. He's always on the "grind." Calvin often went to Detroit Michigan. He'll came back with stacks of money. He bought me clothes, shoes, jewelry and purses. I never had a man do for me like he did for me. I felt that I deserved all the "gifts," he presented me.

I trusted him with my life. Calvin told me many times to stop doing hair. That he'll take care of me, and that no woman of his wasn't going to be some "basement hair stylist." He made me think about my future. I was always fascinated by his intellect. I felt he was very wise. Calvin wanted me to be some body. He thought because I'm such a caring and loving person I should take up, registered nursing like Alyssa. He even insist on paying for my college education. If I was to go to school here in Toledo.

For a seventeen year old I got it going on. I will go to school fresh from head to toe, with a wardrobe that cost as much as my car. People started talking the girls at school became envy, the boys became fearful to talk to me. You wouldn't believe the stares and outburst of insults I encountered. It got so bad that Calvin came up to my school. He had to hem up quite a few guys. Calvin didn't care he grabbed these guys right outside of the school. In front of everybody.

I didn't have to drive because my man wanted me to depend on him one hundred percent. He had his boy Russ driving my car. Calvin told me it turns him on for me to need him. I loved turning him on. I felt so addicted to him. I couldn't image him not being in my life. He makes my heart beat. Even with the confusion I have in school. I can get through it because, "I love him so much!" People in general is just jealous. Calvin said I need to get use to it.

With all this talk about Calvin. My Grandparents wanted to meet him. Calvin came and picked me up to go to the movies. He came in for a brief moment to finally meet my Granny and Poppy. They both said to me, "he sure is good looking." They then communicated with Calvin stating that he was my first boyfriend. They told him I may be young but smart and mature for my age and to not take advantage of me. Calvin replied, "you all have my honesty." "I will be nothing but good to her."

Calvin owl eyed my grandfather's watch. He was amazed by my Poppy's lavish taste of clothing and jewels. Calvin and my Poppy started talking about sports, particularly basketball. My grandfather was a Chicago Bulls fan. Calvin on the other hand was rooting for the L.A. Lakers. He claimed his father was brought up there. My poppy then invited Calvin for a game night. Calvin was pleased to accompany my poppy for a game or two.

CHAPTER FIVE

Graduation.

Finally my last day of school. I will be walking across the stage next Wednesday. All I can think about is my mother. I'm starting to have weary feelings connected to her. I just don't know what it is she wants from me. I know she's around me somehow. Every since I met Calvin three months ago, my life has changed. I haven't had those uncomfortable visions of her death. But I do feel more of her spirit shadowing my life path at this time. I feel my mother wants to communicate with me for some strange reason.

Now that I have Calvin I no longer urge the desire to think about my mother let alone anything else. He was all that mattered and what he wanted for me. I didn't attend my prom, because he didn't want to go. Girls kept telling me he was a cheater. And describing how he had sex with them. I believe my man is good to me. He shows me by all the things he says and do for me. Calvin is right they all wish they had what him and I have. My relationship with friends ended.

One day after coming back from the mall with Calvin. I went over to Alyssa's house to show off my purses, shoes and outfits. I even got my nails done. Calvin said he wants me to keep my nails done. Now that I don't have to do hair. He loved them painted red, as well as my toes. He thought I was the sexy thing alive. Alyssa wasn't impressed with my new things. She thought I was becoming extremely superficial.

She was looking mad and confused. She couldn't hold her feeling inside any longer. Therefore she came to me in all honesty proclaiming, Calvin tried to have sex with her. Alyssa described the night, she was over Calvin's. How Calvin tried to come on to her on their way back from getting pizza and movies. She claimed, that she didn't tell me right away because she knew how much I cared for Calvin. She didn't want to hurt my feelings. She then went on saying, "that's why I came back crying and wanted to go home." "I wasn't crying because I missed Darwin, I was crying because I felt violated."

Calvin denied the accusations, and made threats to Alyssa. Calvin didn't want me talking to her and my other friends. Calvin felt that everybody was jealous of our perfect relationship. But in the back of my mind, I somewhat believed Alyssa. I wish she would of came to me sooner. I feel so confused. Calvin said it was the other way around. Although I loved them both, I mean she was my best friend and he's my man.

My grandparents became very concerned with me and Calvin's serious relationship, so sudden. They were shocked that

I no longer wanted to do hair. My granny was the one of select few heads, I was able to do. Because Calvin pretty much occupied most of my time. Hair was my passion. I guess I'm getting older and wiser.

My poppy had Calvin come over to our house. The Lakers was playing the Bulls. My granny fixed baked chicken, brown rice, collard greens with hot water corn bread. For desert she made her infamous lemon cake. She made some ice cold cherry kool aid, that'll knock your socks off. It was half time, Calvin went to the bathroom. While Calvin was using the bathroom, my grandparents spoke highly of him. They were captivated by his charm and wisdom. For him to be as young as he was, they said he seemed well rounded. They asked me what do he do for a living. I suggest to my grandparents to ask Calvin themselves. They was okay with his age because it was the same difference as their age. We continued our small talk and my poppy cracked jokes on how Calvin must be ripping another hole. in the bathroom. He must have been in there at least ten minutes.

When Calvin came out he was rubbing his stomach, thanking my granny for her delicious meal. He did say the greens got him in the best and worst way. If you know what I mean. We giggled a bit. My grandfather went on and asked Calvin, "what do you do for money?". "He said I hope you're not a dope boy!" "I see you like nice things as I do." "So what do you do?"

Calvin replied, "I have my own businesses." "I'm an independent contractor, that does various real estate transactions." "Flipping houses to construction to being an landlord etc." Calvin continued, "when it comes to real estate you name it, I can do it !" My poppy and Calvin seemed to have some things in common.

Calvin wants me to move in with him after graduation. I had no clue on how I was going to break the news to my grandparents. Calvin bought me a promise ring, and we had dinner at Toledo's finest restaurant. Calvin surprised me by inviting my grandparents out to dinner with us. He told my grandparents he will love to marry me someday, after I complete college.

My grandfather was always into dressing the best. From Calvin's outer exterior he was warmly accepted by my grandfather. My grandmother didn't like the fact of how all my time was being spent with Calvin. It started to interfere with my close relationship with my grandparents. My poppy was on Calvin's side. When my granny would vent to him regarding my relationship with Calvin. My poppy would say, "leave those kids alone, they're in love."

Right after graduation I packed all of my belongings and moved in with Calvin. We were so happy. I cooked every day, I cleaned and I gave him my body like women go through toilet paper. Calvin's sex appetite increase. He made me take it in places I didn't know can be utilized. He was always drinking and smoking. He told me we were made for each other, and he'll die for me. I loved him so much. I just didn't care for all the sex acts he required at times. I'm pretty independent. It seems as though he is robbing me from me.

The visions of my mother is starting to come back. But the same vision I had for her is now me. I see me in death from over dosing. I feel so alone and scared. I don't know what to do. So I decided to talk to Calvin about the loss of my mother. He didn't act as if he really cared. He was more so nonchalant, and told me "too bad." We started talking about his parents. He said his dad name was Craig. He claimed his father was, "The Man," back in Los Angeles, California. He ran an efficient distributing operation there. Calvin said, "my father preferred for me to work under his umbrella." "So by things not working out in Germany, it worked in me and my dad's favor."

Calvin replied that, his dad was much older than his mom. He said his dad wanted him to follow his footsteps. Calvin explained how close he was to his mom. They had a bond like no other. Calvin mom name was Cindy. Calvin was her one and only child. She had him when she was only 14 years old. They had a brother and sister type of relationship. Calvin showed me a picture of him and her at a cabaret. They looked like twins. She's a nice looking lady with a nice petite shape. She was light skin, with black curly hair. I guess that's where Calvin gets his looks. She looked quite wild and sneaky. They basically grew up together.

Cindy worked for a smaller industrial plant, contracted by one of the big 3's. She incorporated the blood of hustling as well. She was a booster, sold bootleg movies, tapes and dinners on Fridays. She was a decent cook. She's married to an older gentleman with money, "of course". She enjoyed getting her drink on. She had a blunt and live wire personality. She spoke freely without hesitation. When I first met her she came off really cool and down to earth. Maybe just a little too down to earth I must say.

She complimented my hair. She was thrilled I did it myself I was rocking pin curls and spiral curls. I was raised to respect my elders. I never swore in the presence of an elder. I referred to Cindy as Mam. What I call her that for she exclaimed, "girl don't be calling me that!" "You make me sound old child". One day while I was doing her hair, she started to freely speak as usual. She was bragging about Calvin. She then said, "you know all my friends use to get with my son." "He loved him some older woman." "That boy was 14 or 15 years old going to bed with grown as woman."

She said it so proudly. I was a little uncomfortable with her demeanor and language she cursed like a drunk sailor. In my mind I thought of that as molestation. Cindy replied, "he was a controlling little joker." "She exclaimed that the older women wasn't having it!" She went on saying, "that's why he turned to the young girls." "He can control yall ass". "He get that shit from his daddy that's why I don't fool with that man no more!" She then laughed, and said "but you a good girl." "Just don't be trying to change no man". Trust me that's how I bumped heads with so many men. Just shut the hell up and do what the man say and you will be okay." "That's why I got me an old cat, he happy long as I meow for him every now and then." She asked if I caught her drift. I just listened and nodded my head. What she said went in one ear and came out the other. That lady was a little touched.

The following Sunday, I went over to see my grandparents. My poppy didn't seem as joyful as usual. They seemed happy to see me. They haven't seen me in some time now. My poppy was under the impression that Calvin may have stolen his watch. He asked me have I seen his stainless steel diamond incrusted Movado limited addition watch. He said he haven't seen it since Calvin and I stopped by. For the game weeks ago. My poppy explained how he had it in the bathroom vanity drawer. My poppy admitted that wasn't the most wisest decision to leave a three thousand dollar watch in the bathroom drawer.

We all agreed that Calvin indeed spent a lot of time in the bathroom, the night he came over. My poppy said he's not blaming anybody. He just want his watch back. I felt bad for my poppy, I'm not use to seeing him upset. I told my granny and poppy Calvin wasn't capable of doing such a thing. My grandparents then ask me if I was happy. I replied, "yes!" We hugged and kissed before I left. I told my grandparents how I love and appreciate them. I told poppy I hope he find his watch.

CHAPTER SIX

College Conflicts.

It's now fall Calvin has taken me to a community college in Toledo to enroll. He paid for my tuition in full. I'm so happy to be back in school. I need to get my mind more on me. I met a few girls, and they think I'm so lucky. Until they realize, I can only communicate with them in school. Calvin said life would be much easier without gossiping women. By me not having a phone and affiliating myself with hating woman. I would be better off living without static. He told me they would just create lies and try to break us up.

The girls from school said Calvin is too controlling. One of the girls was Calvin's age. Her name was Amy Mitchell. Amy was tall and lanky. She wore her hair in box braids shaped into a bob. She was dark brown with big bucked eyes. She often wore sweat shirts and jogging pants. I guess that's why she was all in my mix. I stood out from the rest. My college days I enjoyed dressing more sophisticated. I often wore designer blouses, with rider pants. My ultimate favorite shoe, was my knee high leather black boots.

Amy seemed to know a lot about me. She knew the type of car I had. The color of my car. How old I was and who my man was. Amy seemed to know much more about Calvin. She use to go to school with him. She said she's best friends with his, "other baby momma Stacy." Amy told me Stacy had a little boy by him. She also said Calvin is a notorious dope dealer. She seemed concern for me. She said to watch out he likes to beat his women. I thought that girl was insane. My man wouldn't lye a hand on me. I see why he didn't want me talking to people. Soon after class was over that day. A gang of girls was in my face, telling me how they slept with my man. Some girls even called him in my face.

If things could only get worse. While I was waiting for Calvin to pick me up. Stacy his alleged baby momma, came up to me and confronted me. She told me that her and Calvin still kick it. I was on Fire! When Calvin picked me up I had some words for him. Calvin said the reason he never told me about his son, was because he wasn't sure he was his. I knew he was lying because that boy was spitting image of him. I asked him how did some of the girls, have his telephone number. He replied, "I'm the man out here." And that he had connects that's just a form of networking. Calvin always seemed to say the right thing at the right time. He had answers to everything. That night we went home and made love.

The following day of school, I held my pride and stop talking to people. But Amy wouldn't read between the lines, that I didn't want to be bothered. She asked about his ex-basketball career. I had no comment. She told me her brother was Russ. Russ wasn't on my good side at the time. He had recently got drunk and crashed my car. Russ told her that the reason why Calvin got kicked off the team was because he was smoking joints laced with crack cocaine. She swore he was a druggie. I know Calvin like to drink and get high but, "crack." Hell no!

I didn't even ask Calvin rather or not he used crack cocaine, because I didn't believe it. She told me that's why Stacy don't mess with him like that. She just use him for his money. She then told me that Stacy was an exotic dancer. That's where Calvin met her. She then proceeded to tell me, that Calvin still go to the clubs and mess with a few of the dancers still to this very day. Amy was determined to reveal Calvin's sinister betrayals.

She told me that Calvin was laying up with Stacy right now as we speak. I told her to prove it. Amy owned a white Ford Tempo, four door. We both hopped in and she drove to Stacy's house. Certainly there it was Calvin's pride possession parked comfortable in her drive way. We got out of her car, and walked on the side of the house. We then peeked in the window. Sure enough Calvin was lying in the bed with another woman. My heart instantly shattered.

We rung the door bell. Stacy came to the door. Stacy was brown skin, with decent features her nose looked a bit piggish. Her hair was covered underneath a purple head scarf. She was wearing a light pink sleeveless silk short night gown. The girl had the nerve to have the pink feathered slippers to match. Her family all lived in the same house. Not just her mom or dad, I'm talking aunt's, uncle's and cousins. The house wasn't even that big. I guess they found a way to lay.

Stacy opened the door and asked Amy, "who you got with you?" Amy replied, "oh this Calvin's girl, remember?" Stacy looked at me and said, "how cute." Stacy woke Calvin up and he came to the door. His eyes shot out of his head. He grabbed his shirt and went after me. I went back to Amy's car and he keep telling me, "It's not what you think!" Stacy was laughing historical. She told me Calvin wasn't worth my time. He was a bonafide "hoe." She said, "little girl the best thing you can do for yourself is leave him alone!" "You see I don't want him like that". I just milk him for what he's worth every now and then." She went on saying Calvin wasn't shit!

My mind was racing, I felt everything coming down on me at once. I went back to thinking about my best friend how she was right about Calvin. If he lied about cheating once why wouldn't he do it again. Calvin begged and pleaded for me to get in his car. My tears was running down my face, dripping onto my Guess jeans. My pants looked as if I urinated on myself. I was crushed. Finally I went into a daze. I no longer heard anything or anybody. I looked out the window at Calvin and he looked at me.

He then opened the door on the passenger side, where I was sitting. He grabbed my purse and backpack and put it into his car. I felt like spaghetti. I didn't have the strength to getup. Calvin picked me up and carried me to his car. He then jumped in and pulled off. I just kept asking him "why?" Why me why did he have to do this to me. I called him a liar. I told him I could never trust him. How much I hated him. Calvin just kept telling me, I didn't mean what I was saying. He told me that they set him up. He said, "it's not what it seems." He said, "you didn't see me doing nothing but sleeping." "I wouldn't do anything with that freak." "I just went over there to smoke a blunt with her." "I got sleepy and went to sleep."

The next day I went back to school. When Calvin picked me up he gave me some tickets in an envelope. It was two round trip tickets to Jamaica. I was speech less. We had 3 nights and 4 days of bliss, royalty and good—good love making. I never seen such clear blue water. The ocean was like a dream. The food was great, it reminded me of my mother's cooking. Calvin enjoyed the home grown plant for pot lovers. He said it was the best weed he ever had.

On the last day of our trip Calvin gave me a gift. When I unwrapped it there it was, a beautiful stainless steel Movado watch. He then pulled back his sleeve. He was wearing a pastel striped colored long sleeve button up shirt. When he pushed back his sleeve, there was a diamond incrusted stainless steel Movado watch. He said, "now we are matching, with the his and hers." It resembled my grandfather's watch. I told him my poppy had the same watch and it was missing.

He said those watches was popular and many people had them. I then told him, "I thought that particular watch was a limited addition." He said it must be a coincidence and that he and my poppy shared similar taste. I responded, "so true!" Calvin sure did know how to dress. I gave him a big long hug. I then thanked him for my watch. He told me that time was of the essence. Whatever that mean. He won my heart back and then some. I was starting to believe his story with Stacy now. I do believe he truly loves me.

When we returned back to Calvin's place he had Russ pick up four dozens of roses. When we were at Calvin's door step you could smell the roses aroma. When I walked in, there was the roses bright red sitting on the kitchen table. With a letter Calvin wrote telling me he was sorry and to give him another chance. After all we're not perfect he had my heart. I know he loves me. What is a girl to do but give him another chance.

During the time I spent completing a four year nursing program. Calvin was constantly in and out of town. That allowed me time for me. I would go over to my grandparents for dinner and to talk on the phone. Calvin didn't know that I still kept in contact with Alyssa. She was my best friend. She loved me and no matter what she was happy as long as I was happy. I knew she was also scared for me. She thought Calvin was bad business.

Alyssa was engaged at that time to Darwin. She too was finishing up in school to obtain her nursing degree. She always was joyful and at peace with herself. I often envy her strong will. I wish I was more like her. Head strong, confident and never depended on a man to do for her. She wanted me to come visit her in Tennessee. If only she knew how controlling Calvin really was. She'll be so disappointed in me, for allowing a man to have such power over me.

I enjoy my time apart from Calvin. The little freedom of talking to my grandparents and my best friend, sort of filled a drip in my empty soul. I wonder how life would be if I would have pursued my hair styling dreams. Instead I have a man that's barely home and I'm basically almost done with college in which he paid my way through with dope money. The same poison that killed my mother, and corrupted my father. I feel so stupid. I feel stuck. I should suggest that, Calvin and I should separate for a while.

CHAPTER SEVEN

Raven Life Turns For The Worst.

Calvin returns home from California. Before he could get settled in he received bad news. He got a call from one of his partners from L.A. stating his dad was just indicted on drug charges as well as possession of lethal weapons. I referred my aunt Jill to him. She had sometime cut for Calvin's dad utilizing her expertise. Not to mention she had clout. She became concerned for my affiliation of her client. I denied my true relationship with Calvin. I told her he went to my college.

I've noticed since Calvin's dad went to prison. He changed a lot he spent an unusual amount of time in the bathroom. When he comes out he's snappy, horny and jumpy. I don't know what's up with him lately. I know he worries a lot more than he ever had before. L.A. was his main link of resources for his revenue. Tomorrow I will be graduating from college with my nursing degree. That night I got up enough courage to have a talk with Calvin. I told him we can still be together. But I was ready to move back home with my grandparents. I told him how much I missed being with them.

That's when Calvin snapped he told me he don't even like them. He stated, "your grandmother is fake!" "She know she don't like me and always smiling in my face." He then went on saying how my grandfather falsely accused him of stealing his watch. He then confessed and said, "so what if I did". "Who leaves a watch worth three grand in the dam bathroom. It was either me or somebody else." "That old coon was asking for it." Calvin shamed me for contacting my grandparents constantly. He said, "stop acting like a little girl, you're a grown woman!"

That night was the worst night of my life. He beat me like white on rice. He kicked me so hard in my stomach. I started hemorrhaging from my pelvic area. I bleed so bad he rushed me to the hospital. I never seen him in radical rage his eyes seemed red, glassy and dilated. He acted as if he was on something beyond drinking and smoking weed. His veins was popping out of his head, arms and legs. He told me not to tell anyone what happened. He wanted me to lie to the doctors. He forced me to say I was robbed and beaten. The doctors wasn't buying my statement. The authorities was contacted and questioned me and still I maintained my story. Fearing my life.

I had x-rays taken I was miscarrying. I didn't even know I was pregnant. I was six weeks into the first trimester. Pain struck so far in the depth of my heart. I wish I was that six week old fetus never entering the world. I couldn't even make it to my very own college graduation. That summer I went into a deep depression. Calvin became viciously jealous. He thought me and Russ had something going. I think he just used that as an excuse to justify his beatings. He so faithfully contributed on a daily basis.

I decided to reach out to Calvin's mom Cindy. When I started to talk to her about how her son was treating me. Cindy immediately jumped in a defense. She said."look girl your problems is your problems." "Hell I got my own dam problems, everybody got problems," "You better solve them." She told me to stop making her son mad. Cindy then said, "you can only go through what you allow." "When yo little ass get tired you'll know what to do." "Now don't be calling back with you and Calvin's little B.S. you hear me?" I told her your right.

I felt ashamed that I exposed my filthy laundry to an heartless soul.Calvin started disrespecting me like never before. I was treated like his sex slave. He entertained women in our home with drugs and alcohol. He made me miscarry once again from the daily beatings. After the second baby lost, I started drinking. Alcohol was my outlet. My self existence, my freedom my life was ending before my eyes.

It was time to slow down on the drinking, summer was almost gone. It was time for me to find a job. I filled out applications everywhere. Calvin contacted his uncle Chops. His real name was Lloyd Harris. His nick name was Chops because he loved to talk. He referred me to an opening for a registered nurse afternoon position at Grace Mercy Hospital. Uncle Chops worked there on Wednesdays as a drug abuse and gunshot victims mentor. He was wheelchair bound due to his mouth and affiliation of being a drug distributor. He was shot in the back with an A-K 47. His spine was shattered. His best friend that he grew up with, as a brother turned on him because of jealousy and tried to kill him. Uncle Chops use to be a big time dope dealer. The streets gave him his nickname. He was and still is a gossiper. He claims he's not as bad as he use to be. Even with some experiences certain traits can be well defined within your roots. He did say his mother was a big talker. He also said it runs through the family. Uncle Chops may have had a mouth on him. But he certainly wasn't a liar. That sister Cindy of his sure was a chatter box. If I never heard one.

Uncle Chops knew he was blessed. He felt as though he is here for a purpose and what he went through was for him to mark his journey. His mentor program is called Mind over Matter. He has been working as a mentor advocate for more than 5 years. Uncle Chops was very inspirational. He showed me around the hospital. He knew everybody business. He definitely earned his name.

After landing the job at Grace Mercy Hospital. I got paid starting off 22 dollars an hour. I worked afternoons. I enjoyed my work shift because it allowed me to be away from Calvin. I learned fast that he was nothing, I thought he was. He was just using me as a puppet. I couldn't come and go as I pleased I couldn't even talk on the dam phone. Thank god, for work although I was paid a decent salary. I couldn't enjoy it, because Calvin took me for everything I was worth on pay day. I only had a forty dollar a week allowance for lunch. Most of the time I would just drink that little change up.

Calvin is now a broke wanna be baller. He think he's doing something but his money has gotten tremendously short in a matter of months. He has been spending more than he could afford. Calvin has become the pawn shop, "King." The employee's they knew him by the sound of his car. With his money becoming low and all. As well as his expensive drug addiction. He had no money for his car maintenance. He only needed a tune up and a new muffler. But the drugs was his main priority.

The first thing he pawned was my grandfather's watch. I felt guilty, there's no way I'll ever tell my poppy the truth. He would of harmed Calvin in the worst way. If he had any idea of what I've been through. My granny probably would take me to church and have the pastor lye hands on me to redeem my absent mind. She always thought church was the cure for everything. Every time I talked to her she would pray for me over the phone. She was anointed by the holy spirit. I prayed so much when I was a young child. It seem like prayer didn't work for me. It seemed it pick and choose whom to answer and who to not. I just gave up on it! My prayer request of them all was to have a mother. After Calvin's first pawn all jewels became history. All my purses was turned into cash for his toxic pleasures.

It was a Wednesday, late afternoon. I was filling in for a co-worker. Because Wednesday is my scheduled day off. What do you know I hear a loud man's voice. Just as chattering and blabbering away. It was none other uncle Chops. He noticed me walking the halls. I tried turning a corner, but it was too late. He then exclaimed, "Calvin girl come here!" He asked me if I had some time. I replied "I'm on break I got another 20 minutes what was up?" He noticed my arms of course. It's hard to cover my lower arms, due to my profession. I have a habit of pushing back my sleeves, when I care for patients. I often forget to cover up my marks.

Uncle Chops showed me his office. He was so proud to show off his awards and achievements. He told me how his tragedy became his reality of miracles. He took a liking to martial arts. Uncle Chops said it was a mind stimulator. It taught him how to meditate and self discipline. I suppose that's how he got guns for arms and his chest was massive. You can tell he worked out. His physique formed through his dress shirts. He resembled Calvin and Cindy. Light skin nice hair cut into a tapered fade. Nice dark eyes. His office design was inspired by, Chinese pieces incorporating some African pieces. He had a few mahogany wood African masks he has for protection from evil. He also had a brass piece of art trimed in red. That Chinese piece read life is worth the fight. He also had pictures hung up, with him on a mate with kids that he teaches martial arts to.

Uncle Chops was one of the first black men with his condition to teach and orchestrate a youth program in martial arts. His number one piece of them all was a pair of gold plated chop sticks. They were inside a glass case in the inside pocket of his briefcase. He mention his team gave it to him for Christmas last year. He stated how martial arts was more than a sport. He said it taught disciple of the mind, body and spirit.

He began to speak upon Calvin. He said, "you know I wish I could of been a better role model for my little nephew. I hope you understand, why he is the way he is." He said, look at his momma the, "Apple didn't Fall Far From the Tree". He said, "that boy been through hell so that's all he know." "He use to watch his daddy beat his momma every day. God was trying to give him a better life by playing ball overseas. But them dam drugs got the best of him. I believe that dam daddy of his, made him try it. Back when he was in high school." "He started off lacing his weed. Now that poor boy take it in his nose. And lord knows, however else."

"He is gone!" He exclaimed, that Calvin would say, I'm not hooked he claimed he knew how to control it. Now look at him it controls him." Uncle Chops grabbed me by the hand and looked me into the windows of my soul. He then spoke these words, "Sister all I can say is I wish you Peace, Love and Happiness. You are a grown woman. You know what's right and what's wrong. In life we all have choices. By never forgetting where you came from. You can appreciate your outcome." I then thanked him for his recommendation and his conversation. He was absolutely right.

What do you know time to go back to work. People on my job would snicker when I wore short sleeves and v necks. I was always proclaiming to falling down stairs to accidentally hurting this, and accidentally hurting that. I did take a liking to a gentleman name Jason Thomas. He was funny and he always made me smile. He was as gentle as an angel's feather. I didn't care, he didn't have the finest hair and the most attractive outer appearance. He was a good man. You can tell he was raised right. He thinks with his heart.

I also loved this older woman name Joyce Miller. She worked the morning shift. Joyce didn't mind covering shifts for co-workers from time to time. She reminded me of my mother. I think she felt like a mother figure to me. She often asked about my eating habits. Because I was so god awful thin. The forty dollars a week wasn't enough to eat off of and support my habit. Joyce will see me coming into work, towards the time for her to go and always brought me lunch. Whatever she ate rather it was carry out or leftovers she always made sure I ate.

CHAPTER EIGHT

Will Raven And This Baby Survive?

Six months later, my belly is poking out and I'm having a baby boy. This is the first time in my life I have something special to look forward to. I'm thinking about naming him after my poppy. I try not to visit my granny and poppy. I talk to them most of the time on my breaks when I'm at work. I don't want them to know I'm pregnant just yet. They would be disappointed of me being with child and not married. Calvin said he doesn't mind if I name the little man Ervin. Ms. Cindy definitely wants him to be a junior, or she'll be happy if I name him a name starting with a C.

Calvin is still strung out. But he treats me much better I haven't been beaten in a while. His baby momma Sharon from Detroit drops off his kids. Once she got word I was carrying Calvin's child. Out the blue she became jealous. Since Calvin's money hasn't been like it use to be. Sharon assumed that's why he hasn't been supporting the kids as much. She called and said she had to come to Toledo to visit family and she was going to drop the girls off. She waited weeks before she picked them back up. They missed at least two weeks of school. Sharon claimed she needed a break.

When Kelly and Kate Lynn came into the house they looked adorable. But looks can be deceiving. They both had on the same thing. They were wearing denim jackets with the pants to match. Their hair was braided with colorful beads on the ends of their hair. They looked like Calvin and Sharon mixed. They had their mother's thick course hair. Their daddy's complexion light brown. They had Sharon's light brown eyes. They were also tall for their age. Calvin was happy to see his kids because he have not seen them in a while.

I cut back on drinking months ago. I have a glass of wine every blue moon. The kids were bad as ever. They was 9 year old twin girls with grown women mentality. You can tell they hang around grown folks, more than they should. I could of sworn I've heard them using profanity a few times. The girls thought they was slick. When I would catch them using foul language, they'll make up words that rhymed with what they actually said. I remember combing Kelly's hair. She was sitting on the floor on a pillow. I was sitting on the sofa. I had a hard time getting the comb through her hair. When I used force the comb went through her hair. I accidently punched myself on the right side of my belly with the comb. I was frightened for my baby. He was okay. I could be pretty paranoid at times.

The girls didn't like me. They didn't want me to have a baby with their dad. They felt I was stealing their dad away from them. They were already against me. Because their mom spoke negative towards me. With those girls mouths I know they listen to everything they hear. Sharon had a sharp tongue, on her. The girls were little miniature Sharon's. So there was no clean sleigh from the start. I thought I felt the baby move. The girls wanted to "play," with my belly. Being tired and all from taking care of them, Calvin, and working full time. I just wanted to relax.

Calvin went ballistic he was freshly out the bathroom. He said, "bitch I dare you not to let my kids touch your stomach." He then said "who in the hell you think you is?" He then pushed me into a wall and kneed me in my stomach. Blood immediately trembled down my legs. The EMS had to pick me up this time. I was losing a lot of blood and was going in and out of conscious. My mother came to me in a vision. She had angel wings and said, "baby you don't have to go like this." "GET OUT!" She then told God to give me more time to make things right.

Calvin has threaten my life physically and verbally. I couldn't tell the doctor the truth. Because Calvin was always there. So again this time I lost my well defined baby boy. The doctor told me I will never hold a baby full term. My uterus was severely damaged from all the miscarriages. I was torn into pieces. I just wanted something of my own to love and love me back. Calvin didn't care about me. He told me I wasn't worth nothing and if it wasn't for my job he'll leave me. Calvin, "Mr. Baller," days had seen better. All the drugs and drinking made him slip. And he has been getting high off his own supply. He's been slipping for some time now.

After I was released from the from the hospital. I went home and the kids was laughing at me. I then locked myself in the bathroom and started screaming. Then I dug my nails in my face and scratched my face like a tiger out on the loose. I felt myself breaking down. I didn't have anything to live for. I was ready to end my own life. Again my mom with wings vision came right in my very own eyes. She told me she loves me and most importantly God loves me. Now it's time for me to love me. She told me you're not going to turn out like me. You will be better and your seeds will be better. She told me to look up for my blessings for they are in reach.

Cold chills swooshed through my soul. I felt internal healing. I never felt the holy spirit before in my life. I then empowered my soul with my magic. I told myself I don't know how, but transition for the better was in my path. When I said those words I felt a spiritual connection. I went back to work. I started reading scriptures that Jason would print out for me. Jason would do anything to make me smile. Calvin was in a dark place. He was dark in a death sense. I felt his energy polluting my natural being.

In my core I knew there was more to come, then just this life. I felt God's love and mercy upon me. I started to believe in God more than I ever had. My faith convinced me that God was not going to forsake me. I knew it was just a matter of time. I pondered on scripture Psalms chapter thirty seven. Alyssa called my job every so often I didn't want her to know how bad things really were. Alyssa is now married to Darwin they have a two year old daughter and one on the way. She's still working at a hospital in Nashville, Tennessee.

I wished I could be like her happy and in peace. Cindy made it her business to call Calvin. She heard about me losing the baby. She told him, he need to get off that "shit!" She told him, "you lucky yo ass ain't in jail." "Hell I feel like calling the police on you." She never disciplined nore spoke to him like a mother. She happens to be thirty years too late. Calvin told her, "you ain't been in my business you ain't about to start now." He then went on saying, "you was young as hell when you had me." "My daddy use to whup yo ass when you was pregnant." "I came out fine!" Then he hung up on her face.

Then it hit me. That's why he is so messed up. He was a stressed fetus, that grew into fazes of distress after distress. Is that why God allowed my babies to go with him. Things do happen for a reason. Maybe my kids with Calvin would of created a recycle of generational curses. Cycles from his blood line to mine. I get it now. I accept it just wasn't meant to be. As humans we tend to adapt to our surroundings. It'll eventually became our reality if we let it. In a sense we could become clay, molding into whatever we become expose to. Until we learn we are not alone. It's something magical, powerful, loving and faithful. That something is the creator of the universe. God is really real. It's time I commit to his love. I know I didn't make it out of my circumstances alive for no reason. What is the reason? I desire to keep living and what he has for me shall be given.

The following Sunday I asked Calvin if he could drop me off to my grandparents. He responded yes. He then asked why. I told him my granny wanted me to do her hair. He then asked why I was wearing a skirt. I responded, because after the incident a shirt would be more comfortable then pants. He said, "oh." If I told him I wanted to go to church I'm sure he wouldn't of dropped me off. I had the best time with my granny and poppy. Church was fantastic. I went up to the alter and the pastor prayed for me.

He told me I was in a realm of spiritual horizons. He also said God had a lot of surprises in store for me. He told me not to make plans, that God already made them for me. He also told me, to just follow the spirit.

When we got back from church my poppy was sitting on the sofa in the living room. He turned and looked at me and told me how much he loves me. My granny already had dinner in the making. The aroma of beef stew was marinating the smell throughout the house. It was the best dinner I had in forever. Desert was her sweet apple cobbler with vanilla ice cream. I watched a basketball game with them. Then we played checkers. My granny and poppy was so much fun. We didn't have to go anywhere to be entertained. Just enjoying one another's company was well satisfying.

They didn't once say anything bad about Calvin. They were just happy to see me. Before I left my granny packed me goodie bags. That day was unforgettable, just like them. Their wet kisses on my cheeks was so appreciated. While on the way home I could smell their sweet scent on my cheeks. Calvin tore my granny's food up like it owed him money.

CHAPTER NINE

Is Raven's Workplace The Path Of Her Destiny?

J ason was still a flirt. He even bought me flowers on occasions. If I could I would love to be with him. He is amazing. He really likes me, he always calling me his wife. I'm going to miss him. Today is his last day. He is moving out of state somewhere south. To further his career in the biblical field. It's such a pleasure praying with him on our breaks. He speaks with an anointing tone in his light yet deep voice. I felt a difference.

I'm starting to realize prayer is real. I mean Calvin still is Calvin. He be so poisoned up he pretty much be in his own world lately. He still picked me up and took me to work. He said he wants us to get married. I no longer like, let alone love that man. I wish to god I can get the hell out of this horrific relationship. I now pray every day. I've been feeling the urge to speak with someone. The next day I went to work. Joyce looked me right into my tired ran down eyes. She said, "baby I know what you're going through." She then told me that I will know when my time was up.

That day seemed so . . . . , long. I got bored and called my grandparents. They haven't heard from me or seen me in a while. My father answered the phone and told me they died a month ago from a car accident. He then explained that their remains has been cremated and on the fireplace mantel. I had enough my time was up. I was dead spiritually. I was ready to live. I missed my granny and poppy. I hope they'll forgive me. I'm so sorry. I wish Joyce or Jason was here. My supervisor ask for me to go home. I panicked and told her, NO! She then held me and whispered, "It's time".

I sat down at my desk, and asked myself how I was going to escape from my sick situation. Something told me to call my best and only friend Alyssa. When she heard my voice she knew I was in danger. She knew I was in danger a long time ago. She was just waiting for me, to tell her the truth. It was time. After confessing my painful and embarrassing circumstances.

Alyssa begged for me to come visit her. I told her, I worked every day as a nurse and is as broke as a pan handler. Alyssa sent for me via western union, the next day I woke up feeling a glow. Angels was smiling down on me. I got dressed like this was my last time ever getting dressed, sleeping, and living under the same roof as Calvin Cook. I felt somewhat for filled in my spirit. While in the car on my way getting dropped off for work. I was wondering how I was going to get to western union. I needed away to pick up the money, Alyssa sent me to visit her in Tennessee. I just so happened to have not even a pretty red penny.

Today was my 25th birthday. It was a Saturday July 17th. I had no idea today was my birthday. My favorite co-worker Joyce Miller remembered. She had a personal cake just for me. She bought cupcakes for everybody else to enjoy. She also had a card. The card was beautiful. Everybody signed my birthday card. Some people even left their telephone numbers, referencing to stay in touch. Weird, no one ever really spoke to me. Why would they give me their number and want to stay in touch? Any who, I received a 360 dollar collection, from all my co-workers. "Happy Birthday to me!" I haven't been this ecstatic for ages. I felt a good change coming my way. For one thing I know is "360," is truly a blessed number. It represents life new beginnings, and changing of cycles.

God gave my mother her wings right before I turned 25 years old. The same age she was when she passed away. The enemy was after my soul. He almost got me a few times. I thank god for allowing my mother to assist me with mending my soul. Before I ended my life like hers. I took my birthday money, put it into my bra and cried like a baby. I then went on my computer and submitted a leave of absence to human resources. My supervisor insisted that I leave early, do to it being my birthday. I took her up on her offer that time.

I immediately caught a cab and went to western union and got on a train and headed straight to Tennessee. While on the train I started thinking about my mother, god and myself. I was probably one of the happiness individuals on planet earth. I didn't have a pot to piss in or a window to through it out of. I only had what I was wearing, blue scrubs and a jacket. I didn't own a purse, they were sold for drugs and alcohol. God has really pulled me together this time. I'm so blessed I can breathe today, I can see today, I can hear today and I am free today! I discreetly continued to pray, cry and praise God.

A middle aged down to earth lady accompanied me while traveling. Her name was, "Gloria," like my mother's name. We both were on our way to Tennessee. Spiritually she was an evangelist and prayed for me. That lady started to prophesized to me. She told me I was told I will never bare children. She said, "but oh, the enemy is a liar." She began to reveal to me that I was going to have a boy and a girl. She implied that my husband is in existence. She also said that I have new life changes for the good and eternity. She invited me to her church once I became settled. I felt so comfortable with Gloria, like I could trust her. She even resembled my mother. I asked her why she was going to Tennessee. She said because her son recently moved there. He had unfinished business to take care of and he had to work. Therefore she was being of her son's support.

Officially there I was, standing on the front porch of Alyssa's house. I said to myself, "Sweet Tennessee." I just wanted to kiss the ground. My fingers couldn't reach the doorbell fast enough. I then rang the doorbell. Alyssa her daughter and husband embraced me. Her home and family was beautiful. Extreme happiness glowed through my being. I never been that happy ever in my life. Alyssa had my own little room set up for me all nice and pretty. Immediately Alyssa advised me to go to spiritual counseling. Alyssa told me when I was ready, she had a job set up for me in the medical field.

Alyssa and I talked a while catching up on the good old times. Sunday came before entering church with Alyssa and her family. I saw beautiful creations of nature. I saw a huge fluffy yellow butterfly, and gorgeous baby blue jays flying in the crisp warm summer air. When entering the church I followed a familiar voice. The speaker happened to be, "Gloria." I was amazed. She spoke great things and delivered a powerful sermon.

After service, I met some of the church members, in a line and shook hands. The last hands there was to shake stood, "Mr. Jason Thomas." I was as thrilled and shocked to see him as he was to see me. Gloria came over to introduce her son to me not knowing we already knew each other. We stayed in contact, during my healing process. Jason and I promised each other, we'll stay in contact with one another.

While I was in the midst of soul searching. I had to put my mind, body and soul on a paradise cleanse. I went weeks without eating meat. I drank only water. My being was going through a retreat. I never had such balance. I felt my body healing inside and out. I was able to think much clearer. I felt love vibrations in my world. Love is all I knew. Because of that it was one thing I must do. I finally loved on my father by forgiving him. I set free my abundance of victories.

The only relative I was closer to was my aunt Jill that lived in New York. Recently she contacted me. She told me I was a fortunate woman. She then explained to me that my grandparents left their life insurance, all of their financial assets as well as their residential properties to me. I fell to the floor, with my face full of tears of joy.

It wasn't long before me and Jason became an item and got married. I never knew God would love me so much, and bless me with life, and pure love. In the beginning of our relationship it was hard for me to cope with the reality of happiness and love. But God revealed to me, that I am deserving. My husband is my gift from God. Our children Jason Ervin Thomas Jr and Nevaeh Gloria Thomas is living and loving god's true gifts. I now possess what I've always dreamed of and that's Peace of Mind, and a Mother.

I decided I no longer wanted to work in the medical field. I wanted to do something to give back to God. I wanted to bless others as God has blessed me. I'm the founder and creator of a non for profit called I S.A.L.E. (Self, Awareness, Learning, Evolution). My Non for profit organization is based on reality. So many people and the youth are so caught up on the name brands, celebrities, sexuality and greed of money. I S.A.L.E. was established to promote people to be individuals and to "Sale" their intellect, creativity and self respect.

I began to mentor people of all ages. The members of my organization was grateful for the opportunity to work with me. Being able to inspire people to embrace their individuality. We made an international movement. I've received several awards and recognitions. The most thing I'm proud of in my position God lead me to. Is to take my life experience and make an impact on the world.

I finally realize, "Is a Rotten Apple Sweet?" Ask yourself that question. For you can't help the tree that you come from. But you can decide which fruits to digest. You can sow a new harvest. You will plant the seeds that you bare. Always know "Everything is in divine order.

And for those wondering what happened to Calvin. While talking to Michelle back in Ohio, she said he was found in his apartment dead from an over dose. Cindy is now a mentor for her brother's organization, Mind Over Matter non for profit. Not taking her son's death in vain. Like Uncle Chops said, "By Never Forgetting Where You Come From, You Can Appreciate Your Outcome!"

The End.

"Set Me Free",

I asked God why, why me?
How come I can't just be me.

I need to be where I want to be,
To embrace my true self and my destiny.

I'm not asking for expensive Tiffany.
I simply want to be Happy.

Set me free, from lack of love, respect and loyalty.
I just want to set free my creativities.

Which is the main element of my creation.
I want to live life happy in this nation.

I thought life was suppose to be amazing,
Instead I become contaminated, and feel almost alienated.

My time of victories is no longer,
Going to be fictional memories.

I will come out free on top,
Mean while the enemy is waiting for me to drop.

I will not give up that easily.
For I am of God's great species.

Believe me I have strong will power.
I will remain sweet refusing to turn sour.

I ask for the negativity to be released. Set free,
And I become royal, call me her majesty.

Rising high, high on cloud nine.
That would be so mighty fine and divine.

Depending on the weather. The clement of my life's atmosphere of
greatness, freshness, and renewal,

I refuse to become a victim of not utilizing my God's
Giving tools.

As a legendary others will feed off of my life treasures.
For I cherish my life. I will not let go. I have more to pour,

And more to grow.
I'm now set free, I thank you for letting me be me!

"The Vibrations of my Creations",

Aligns me within the depths of my core,
That's the main element that gives,
Me light and so much more.

It's a feel that gives me fume,
And allows my creativity to bloom.

The vibrations of my creation,
Breathes breathe in my existence,
I gravitate on life for its not to be resisted.

I'm in tune with my being.
I enjoy the essence of seeing.
Life is so divine filled with love,
As bright as the sunshine.

For I am grateful for many fruits.
I embrace the grace of the blessed,
Vibrations of my nature,
That completes my security,
Of righteous being my alumni.

If it wasn't for the directions of my vibrations,
I don't know where I'll be,
I just appreciate being able to live life free.

I thank God for me.

"The Feel of Confusion",

Is it an illusion? Or can it be the
Thought of losing . . . . ,

Something that's meant to be or
Shall, I say not meant to be.

What can it be?
The thought of not knowing,
The thought of not claiming my destiny,
Is putting me into misery.

Yeah . . . , the thought of confusion,
Is a state I'll rather not demonstrate,

This feel, because it only kills . . . ,
Integrity, my dignity, my well-being.

And, that feel is ill to my character.
I have much more to live for.

Rather than the feel of confusion.
It is pollution to my soul.

I control this feel, only I know
This is not me it's not real.

I have mighty power of my soul,
With only one main control,

That gives me, my strength,
My courage and wisdom.

I must come back to the true me,
Learn me, teach me, and love me.

And that's when the confusion will be set free!

"Dang daddy where are you?"

When It's cold and my feelings are blue,
When I feel sad and don't know what to do,
When I need fatherly support and love,
You're the one I'm thinking of,

"Dang daddy where are you?"
When I'm feeling down,
In my heart a void from you is bound,
When I look for you, you're no where to be found.

"Dang daddy where are you?"
When I'm feeling no smile,
Where are you to make my life worth while,
I need to look at you as a role model,
You is the man I'm suppose to follow,
Instead you leave my heart bruised and hollow,

"Dang daddy where are you?"
When I feel no liberty,
Where is your positive energy,
I love you Daddy, Do you love me, I can't see,
You have to show me and take on you responsibilities.

"Red Sea,"

Red Sea where would I be . . . ,
Red Sea set me free . . . ,
Red Sea is a part of me . . . ,
Red Sea flows through my vessels of existence,
Red Sea so easy to reach for it dwells is my spirit,
Red Sea is meant to be for you shall not fear it,
Red Sea is everything it's my connection to power,
Red Sea cleanses me, and forgives me for my sins,
Red Sea is of God's divine plans,
Red Sea will carry me to my destiny,
Red Sea in bodies me for life's purpose,
Red Sea will take me to my heavenly destinations,
Red Sea is the mission of the blood of Jesus, whom put me into position,
Red Sea allows me to gradually transition,
Red Sea hears me forever it listens,
Red Sea needs me to share the blood of love,
Red Sea uses me to fill the sea with eyes that see,
Red Sea has granted me promises from above.

"A Mother's Love",

When I think of mother I think of love,
Giving the birth right of living.
On this day I give thanksgiving,

Being a mother is such a wonderful gift,
We're here as a shoulder,
In our children we lift,

Baring life for what it's worth,
While standing in the high,
Walking path of this magical earth,

For we endure many life circumstances,
Living in righteous gives us our power,
To endower whatever comes our way,

In our hearts the piece that meets,
The very lining of our children's feet,
For we are created to structure our creations,

That's manifested in our beings,
For I know there's more to this life,
Then just what is seen,

If you know our King and the works of his arts,
Looking at our children reveals the mission,
Of his heart,

In his love may we never depart.
Children are miracles and the testament of our life.
On each day may we all give thanks to Christ.

"Is a Rotten Apple Still Sweet?"

The taste of many,
Coming from trees of infinity,

It's a form of textures of life,
And what it could be,

Sweet or sour,
The energy you possess,
Will determine your power,
And measures of success,

We must confess the rotten limbs of our fruit,
To plant new seeds,
Of nutrients of what the spirit needs,

We must not feed into what's not good for you,
But feed into a harvest of abundance.

Apples are to be of the eye,
Bringing forth renewals in life,

That will set your heart free,
Pumping divine vessels of victory,

Truth is in the tree,
In it we are set free,

Calling on oxygen,
I now can breathe.

"My heart Bleeds Ink",

From every word I speak,
To what my mind thinks.

My Heart Bleeds Ink,
To every heart beat,
It's what my soul eats.

My Heart Bleeds Ink,
Through every eye blink,
Self awareness of being unique,
My passion giving reverence to sink.

My Heart Bleeds Ink,
Reed is the utensil,
That bleeds in my blood vessels,
It allows my being to flow through my temples,
Sheading light, of an expression on black and white.

My heart Bleeds Ink,
It travels from ancestors to me,
To the still waters so deep,
I come from the cattle of the righteous sheep.

My Heart Bleeds Ink,
It generates many forms of art,
Evolution of geographic body parts,
Ink of ever lasting permanent marks.

My Heart Bleeds Ink,
Unveiling promised memories,
Recordence of our beautiful history.

ABOUT THE AUTHOR

"Red Angel" is a Michigan native, from the Detroit Metropolitan area. She discovered her passion for writing at the early age of seven. She used writing as a healing token when she incurred life pains and disappointments. Angel enjoys being a home body and sharing God's love with people. She's happily married with two beautiful daughters. Her inspiration comes from her center core. She's gifted by our creator, and utilizes her blessings to reach closer to others. She loves to write by all means, children books, novels, scripts, poetry and speeches. She embraces life as it comes, sweet as the golden sun. On her free time she likes to travel and explore nature.

Angel prefers to be referred to as the title "Red Angel", as her expression of the "Angel of Love", in referencing her authoring and artistic projects.

~Contact the Author~
Promisesofpower@gmail.com